This Walker book belongs to:

_____

_____

First published 1987
by Walker Books Ltd, 87 Vauxhall Walk, London SE11 5HJ

This edition published 2016

2 4 6 8 10 9 7 5 3 1

This book has been typeset in Bembo

Printed in China

British Library Cataloguing in Publication Data:
a catalogue record for this book is available from the British Library

ISBN 978-1-4063-7208-3

www.walker.co.uk

Hard-boiled Legs

The Breakfast Book

Michael Rosen   Quentin Blake

WALKER BOOKS
AND SUBSIDIARIES

LONDON · BOSTON · SYDNEY · AUCKLAND

Breakfast Time

Someone's dropped a bottle of milk,
the dustman's dropped a dustbin.

Someone's found a piece of potato in their shoe,
the baby's eating a sock.
When is it?
Breakfast time.

The cat's on the table eating someone's bacon,
someone's wiped butter on their trousers.
Someone's poured tea into the sugar bowl,
the baby is eating eggshells.
When is it?
Breakfast time.

Someone thinks they're going to get very angry,
someone thinks they're going crazy.
Someone thinks they're going to scream,
the baby has tipped cornflakes over its head.
When is it?
Breakfast time.

What If...

What if
a piece of toast turned into a piece of ghost
just as you were eating it
and you thought you were going to sink your
teeth into a lovely crunchy piece of hot toast
and butter and instead this cold wet feeling
jumps into your mouth
going,
"Whoooooooooooooooooooo!"
right down into your stomach

and your mum says,
"What did you say?"
You say, "Nothing, Mum,"
but the ghost sitting in your stomach
does it again.
"Whooooooooooooooooooooo!"
and everyone looks at you.

Things We Say

A Little Boy Came Down to Breakfast

A little boy came down to breakfast
with bananas stuck in his ears.

Everyone said hello to him
but he didn't take any notice.
So his mum said, "Are you all right?"
but the little boy said nothing.
So his sister said, "Are you all right?"
but the little boy still said nothing.

Then his brother noticed that he had bananas stuck in his ears, so he said, "Hey, you've got bananas stuck in your ears," and the little boy said, "What?" So his brother said it again. "You've got bananas stuck in your ears," and the little boy said, "What?" So the brother shouted really loudly at him, "YOU'VE GOT BANANAS STUCK IN YOUR EARS!" And the little boy shouted back, "I'M SORRY, I CAN'T HEAR YOU. I'VE GOT BANANAS IN MY EARS!"

Nat and Anna

Nat and Anna were having breakfast.
Mum said to Anna, "I'm just going upstairs
to get ready. Make sure Nat finishes his
breakfast, will you?"

Mum went out.
Nat got off his chair.
Anna said, "Sit down, Nat."
Nat said, "I'm going for a walk."
Anna said, "Sit down, Nat."
Nat came back and sat down.
Nat said, "I sat down, Anna. Can I get up now?"
Anna said, "Sit down, Nat."
Nat said, "I'm going to the beach."
Anna said, "Sit down, Nat."

Nat went under the table and sat down.
Nat said, "I'm sitting down now, Anna."
Anna said, "You can't sit there, Nat."
Nat said, "I'm having a picnic at the beach."
Anna said, "But you haven't got a picnic with you."
Nat came out from under the table and sat down
on his chair.

Mum shouted from upstairs,
"Are you all right?"
Anna said, "Yes."

Nat got off the chair with a bowl of cornflakes.
Anna said, "What are you doing?"
Nat said, "I'm going to the beach with a picnic."
Anna said, "Sit down, Nat."

Nat got under the table and sat down with a
bowl of cornflakes.

Nat said, "I'm sitting down having my picnic
at the beach."

Anna said, "I'm going to pull you out of there, Nat."

Nat said, "You can't. You're not on the beach."

Anna said, "I can. Look."

Anna pulled Nat very hard.

The cornflakes and milk spilt all over the floor.

Mum shouted from upstairs,
"Everything all right?"

Nat said, "No."

Anna said, "You're going to get into trouble
now, Nat."

Mum came in.

Mum said, "What is going on? What's all this mess all over the floor?"

Nat said, "We're having a picnic at the beach, aren't we, Anna?"

Mum said, "Listen here, Anna. Next time I leave you alone like that, don't get Nat playing your silly games, do you understand? Now go to your room and stay there."

Anna walked out.

Nat said, "Can I go with her?"

Mum said, "No."

Anna said, "No no no no no no no no no no no."

Nat said, "Why's Anna shouting?"

What Happens Next?

If he treads on the dog…

If the dog tries to run…

If the table moves…

If the parrot…

If the man up the ladder…

OH NO! OH NO! OH NO!

What If…

What if

hard-boiled eggs turned into hard-boiled legs

just when your dad was eating his egg

and he says,

"Hey, what's this?"

and the hard-boiled leg starts to run all round

the table and your dad starts to chase it.

"I want my egg!"

but the leg stands up and says,

"You can't catch me,

I'm no egg.

You can't catch me,

I'm a hard-boiled leg,"

and it runs out the door and your dad runs out
the door after it,
still wearing his pyjamas.

About the Author

Michael Rosen is one of the most popular authors of stories and poems for children. His titles include *We're Going on a Bear Hunt* (winner of the Smarties Book Prize), *Little Rabbit Foo Foo*, *Tiny Little Fly* and *Dear Mother Goose*. He has written many collections of poetry including *Let's Get Out of Here* and *Don't Put Mustard in the Custard*, both illustrated by Quentin Blake. He also compiled *Classic Poetry: An Illustrated Collection*. In 1997 he received the Eleanor Farjeon Award for services to children's literature and in 2007 he was appointed Children's Laureate.

About the Illustrator

Quentin Blake is a critically acclaimed children's book artist and was voted "The Illustrator's Illustrator" by *Observer* magazine. He is the illustrator of numerous Roald Dahl titles, several Michael Rosen poetry collections, *Michael Rosen's Sad Book* and *The Rights of the Reader* by Daniel Pennac. He has also created many acclaimed picture books of his own, including *Mr Magnolia* (winner of the Kate Greenaway Medal), *All Join In* (winner of the Kurt Maschler Award) and *Clown* (winner of Bologna Ragazzi Prize). In 1999 he was appointed the first Children's Laureate and in 2005 he was awarded a CBE for services to children's literature.